"Repent, Harlequin!" Said the Ticktockman

NOVELS

WEB OF THE CITY [1958]   THE SOUND OF A SCYTHE [1960]   SPIDER KISS [1961]

DEMON WITH A GLASS HAND (ADAPTATION WITH MARSHALL ROGERS) [1986]

NIGHT AND THE ENEMY (ADAPTATION WITH KEN STEACY) [1987]

VIC AND BLOOD: THE CHRONICLES OF A BOY AND HIS DOG (ADAPTATION WITH RICHARD CORBEN) [1989]

HARLAN ELLISON'S DREAM CORRIDOR VOLUME 1 [1996]

SHORT NOVELS

DOOMSMAN [1967]   ALL THE LIES THAT ARE MY LIFE [1980]

RUN FOR THE STARS [1991]   MEFISTO IN ONYX [1993]

SHORT STORY COLLECTIONS

THE DEADLY STREETS [1958]   SEX GANG [1959] (AS PAUL MERCHANT)

A TOUCH OF INFINITY [1960]   CHILDREN OF THE STREETS [1961]

GENTLEMAN JUNKIE AND OTHER STORIES OF THE HUNG-UP GENERATION [1961]

ELLISON WONDERLAND [1962]   PAINGOD AND OTHER DELUSIONS [1965]

I HAVE NO MOUTH & I MUST SCREAM [1967]   FROM THE LAND OF FEAR [1967]

LOVE AIN'T NOTHING BUT SEX MISSPELLED [1968]

THE BEAST THAT SHOUTED LOVE AT THE HEART OF THE WORLD [1969]

OVER THE EDGE [1970]

DE HELDEN VAN DE HIGHWAY [1973] (DUTCH PUBLICATION ONLY)

ALL THE SOUNDS OF FEAR [1973] (BRITISH PUBLICATION ONLY)

THE TIME OF THE EYE [1974] (BRITISH PUBLICATION ONLY)

APPROACHING OBLIVION [1974]   DEATHBIRD STORIES [1975]

NO DOORS, NO WINDOWS [1975]

HOE KAN IK SCHREEUWEN ZONDER MOND [1977] (DUTCH PUBLICATION ONLY)

STRANGE WINE [1978]   SHATTERDAY [1980]

STALKING THE NIGHTMARE [1982]   ANGRY CANDY [1988]

ENSAMVÄRK [1992] (SWEDISH PUBLICATION ONLY)   JOKES WITHOUT PUNCHLINES [1995]

ВСЕ ЗВУКИ СТРАХА (ALL FEARFUL SOUNDS) [1997] (UNAUTHORIZED RUSSIAN PUBLICATION ONLY)

THE WORLDS OF HARLAN ELLISON [1997] (AUTHORIZED RUSSIAN PUBLICATION ONLY)

SLIPPAGE [1997]   ROUGH BEASTS [FORTHCOMING]

OMNIBUS VOLUMES

THE FANTASIES OF HARLAN ELLISON [1979]   DREAMS WITH SHARP TEETH [1991]

THE WHITE WOLF SERIES:

EDGEWORKS 1 [1996]   EDGEWORKS 2 [1996]   EDGEWORKS 3 [1997]   EDGEWORKS 4 [1997]

COLLABORATIONS

PARTNERS IN WONDER SF COLLABORATIONS WITH 14 OTHER WILD TALENTS [1971]
THE STARLOST: PHOENIX WITHOUT ASHES (WITH EDWARD BRYANT) [1975]
MIND FIELDS 33 STORIES INSPIRED BY THE ART OF JACEK YERKA [1994]

NON-FICTION & ESSAYS

MEMOS FROM PURGATORY [1961]
THE GLASS TEAT ESSAYS OF OPINION ON TELEVISION [1970]
THE OTHER GLASS TEAT FURTHER ESSAYS OF OPINION ON TELEVISION [1975]
THE BOOK OF ELLISON (EDITED BY ANDREW PORTER) [1978]
SLEEPLESS NIGHTS IN THE PROCRUSTEAN BED ESSAYS (EDITED BY MARTY CLARK) [1984]
AN EDGE IN MY VOICE [1985]   HARLAN ELLISON'S WATCHING [1989]
THE HARLAN ELLISON HORNBOOK [1990]

SCREENPLAYS, ETC.

THE ILLUSTRATED HARLAN ELLISON (EDITED BY BYRON PREISS) [1978]
HARLAN ELLISON'S MOVIE [1990]
I, ROBOT: THE ILLUSTRATED SCREENPLAY (BASED ON ISAAC ASIMOV'S STORY-CYCLE) [1994]
THE CITY ON THE EDGE OF FOREVER (1995/1996)
"REPENT, HARLEQUIN!" SAID THE TICKTOCKMAN (RENDERED WITH PAINTINGS BY RICK BERRY) [1997]

RETROSPECTIVES

ALONE AGAINST TOMORROW A 10-YEAR SURVEY [1971]
THE ESSENTIAL ELLISON A 35-YEAR RETROSPECTIVE [1987]
(EDITED BY TERRY DOWLING, WITH RICHARD DELAP & GIL LAMONT)

AS EDITOR

DANGEROUS VISIONS [1967]
NIGHTSHADE & DAMNATIONS: THE FINEST STORIES OF GERALD KERSH [1968]
AGAIN, DANGEROUS VISIONS [1972]
MEDEA: HARLAN'S WORLD [1985]
THE HARLAN ELLISON DISCOVERY SERIES:
AUTUMN ANGELS [1975] BY ARTHUR BYRON COVER   STORMTRACK [1975] BY JAMES SUTHERLAND
THE LIGHT AT THE END OF THE UNIVERSE [1976] BY TERRY CARR
ISLANDS [1976] BY MARTA RANDALL
INVOLUTION OCEAN [1978] BY BRUCE STERLING

"Repent, Harlequin!" Said the Ticktockman

the classic story by
Harlan Ellison
illustrated by
Rick Berry

designed by
Arnie Fenner

UNDER WOOD BOOKS

G r a s s   V a l l e y ,   C A
1 9 9 7

"REPENT, HARLEQUIN!" SAID THE TICKTOCKMAN

Dedicated to *Sheila Berry.*
I'd like to extend my thanks to Darrel Anderson, Bill Eidson, and Cathy and Arnie Fenner
for their help and encouragement throughout this project.
R.B.

PLATES

frontis: " ...and one day we no longer let time serve us, we serve time and we are slaves of the schedule..."

page 8: Deco Clock

page 18: "Even in the cubicles of the hierarchy, where fear was generated, seldom suffered, he was called the Ticktockman. But no one called him that to his mask."

page 23: "The System had been seven minutes' worth of disrupted."

page 27: ' "You know," Pretty Alice noted, "you speak with a great deal of inflection." '

pages 30 & 31: "...and of course the authorities were there, lying in wait for him."

page 34: "And early the next day, when turn-off time came, he was deep in the Canadian forest two hundred miles away..."

page 38: ' "Scare someone else. I'd rather be dead than live in a dumb world with a bogeyman like you." '

Jacket, book, and typography design by Arnie Fenner.

Printed in Hong Kong
FIRST EDITION
10 9 8 7 6 5 4 3 2 1

Signed Limited Edition/October 1997 ISBN 1-887424-36-9
Trade Edition/October 1997 ISBN 1-887424-35-0

Library of Congress Cataloging-in-Publication Data
Ellison, Harlan.
   "Repent, Harlequin!" said the Ticktockman : the classic story / by
Harlan Ellison ; illustrated by Rick Berry. -- 1st ed.
      p.   cm.
   On t.p. the "o" in Ticktockman appears as a clock.
   ISBN 1-887424-35-0 (hardcover). -- ISBN 1-887424-36-9 (signed
limited ed.)
   I. Title.
PS3555.L62R46   1997
813' .54--dc21   97-26744
                                                          CIP

Underwood Books, P.O. Box 1609, Grass Valley, CA 95945
For a current catalog please send a stamped, self-addressed envelope to the above address.

*This one, sent with love and
endless friendship, to Susan's and my
dear chum & pal, the svelte
and nonpareil sweetie,*

ANNE McCAFFREY

Stealing Tomorrow

HARLAN ELLISON

My soul would be an outlaw. I can do nothing with it.

The coward body my soul inhabits has pleaded with the renegade, has cried for pity, has implored the pistolero, my soul, to live safely, to observe quietly, to live in peace, with a degree of contentment.

My soul curses like the guttersnipe it is, and hurls another Molotov cocktail at my complacency. So I am doomed. My soul *will be* an outlaw. It will be Zorro, dressed in black, carving its initials in the sane and rational. It will be Jean Lafitte, stalking through the Louisiana swamps of my days and nights, prepared to defend my cringing, cowardly self from the invaders called compromise. It will be a coocoo Charlie Chaplin, hurling a pie at whatever it takes to live quietly, sensibly, safely.

And here am I, trapped in the body with this dangerous, feral outlaw, who seems determined to alienate, to upset, to annoy, to harass and chivy and unsettle me.

I lust for the day when soul transplants come to be.

For my soul, the masked *bandido*, is a dreamer. He is engaged in the biggest caper of them all. I take this moment (while the soul is out on one of its forays against the decent and proper folk of the world), to set down and relate its plans. To apprise you that the outlaw Attilla Genghis Khan John Brown marauder is planning the greatest theft of all time.

My mad soul would steal tomorrow.

He would wrest tomorrow from the jaws of today and turn it topsy-turvy. He would come lumbering into town on a pink-and-yellow elephant, fast as Pegasus, and throw down on the established order. At gunpoint, the depraved and lunatic soul would order that tomorrow be handed over, and then, wheeling, gallop off, back to his lair in the Rainbow Plaid Mountains, where he would hold tomorrow hostage, raping and pillaging her, till her brains turned to cotton candy.

I hasten to assure you, I am no party to this depravity. I am a quiet country boy merely trying to make a peaceful way in the world. It is this outlaw soul of mine who is the trouble-maker.

And I can only repeat what he says about his motivations, in hopes someone can arrive in time to thwart his nefarious plans.

What my soul says is this:

Anthropologists tell us that from what they have been able to ascertain, from skulls found in caves at Baden, Germany, that the "reasoning" section of the human brain, the cerebellum of modern man, is many times larger than that of the primates. But the situs containing the emotions—the medulla—is precisely the same size. We have become creatures capable of sending rockets to the moon, capable of probing the bottom of the oceans, capable of computing and assaying and estimating and dreaming. But we are still naked apes when our emotions are excited.

My soul says: tomorrow cannot be trusted to naked apes. My soul seems to think he is Robin Hood, stealing from the ill-equipped to give to the as-yet-unborn. I cannot argue with my soul; it will hear no counter-suggestion. So what am I to do? I'm trapped here with the slobbering degenerate.

My soul says he has received "the call." That he has been touched by the Maker. (And I fear to ask him *which* Maker, or *what* Maker, for fear he will tell me . . . and I don't want to know, not really!) A peculiar assertion from the soul of a contented Atheist.

My soul, in his more rational moments, tells me that he will cease raiding when, and only when, folks come to realize that all other folks are noble. He tells me he will lie back and let the world handle itself only when color and creed and race and religion cease being interfaces between other men. He says he has had "the call" and his mission is to keep the posse out looking for him, because that will keep them aware of the fact that not everyone can be sold into slavery quite so easily, and that in this day and age "holy wars" are imbecile activities.

You can see my situation. My problem is one of helplessness. I mean no ill, I mean no offense. It is this carnivorous soul, this Mr. Hyde in my eminently sane and rational Dr. Jekyll body.

If you want *my* opinion, my soul is bad-to-the-bone crazy. I don't think charmingly crazy, like one of the Marx Brothers; I mean stoned righteously crazy, with a lack of humility, without a vestige of reverence, without a response in him that would keep him prudent, lead-lined safe, and following along the way others should follow. I think he ought to be locked up. I think they ought to throw away the key. Hell, I'll rat him out: I hope the posse catches him. That's what *I* hope.

But he's cunning, you see. He comes equipped with dreams, and they're weapons of frightful potency. He uses them shamefully, if you ask me. He rails against the most sensible directives from the world, he curses those who set the rules, he refuses to listen or accept even the most rational reasons for the most sensible acts.

Let me give you a for instance.

My soul is never on time.

If my soul tells you he'll be there at seven o'clock, look for him next Thursday. He flaunts the rigors and rules of punctuality, and when I insist that he is once again shaking up the natural order of things, he sticks out his tongue, he shoots me the finger, he uses one of his dreams on me.

Let me tell you about that mocking dream…

Because my soul says Thoreau was right when he said: "He serves the State best who opposes the State most" (if you want my opinion, Thoreau's soul was an outlaw, too), here is the dream my soul tells:

"Repent, Harlequin!" Said the Ticktockman

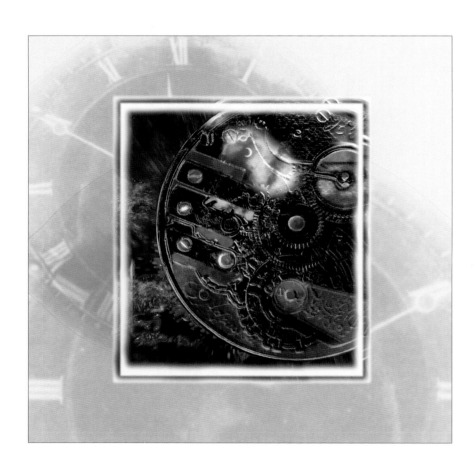

There are always those who ask, what is it all about? For those who need to ask, for those who need points sharply made, who need to know "where it's at," this:

> *The mass of men serve the state thus, not as men mainly, but as machines, with their bodies. They are the standing army, and the militia, jailers, constables,* posse comitatus, *etc. In most cases there is no free exercise whatever of the judgment or of the moral sense; but they put themselves on a level with wood and earth and stones; and wooden men can perhaps be manufactured that will serve the purpose as well. Such command no more respect than men of straw or a lump of dirt. They have the same sort of worth only as horses and dogs. Yet such as these even are commonly esteemed good citizens. Others—as most legislators, politicians, lawyers, ministers, and officeholders—serve the state chiefly with their heads; and, as they rarely make any moral distinctions, they are as likely to serve the Devil, without intending it, as God. A very few, as heroes, patriots, martyrs, reformers in the great sense, and* men, *serve the state with their consciences also, and so necessarily resist it for the most part; and they are commonly treated as enemies by it.*
>
> Henry David Thoreau
> *Civil Disobedience*

That is the heart of it. Now begin in the middle, and later learn the beginning; the end will take care of itself.

But because it was the very world it was, the very world they had allowed it to *become,* for months his activities did not come to the alarmed attention of The Ones Who Kept The Machine Functioning Smoothly, the ones who poured the very best butter over the cams and mainsprings of the culture. Not until it had become obvious that somehow, someway, he had become a notoriety, a celebrity, perhaps even a hero for (what Officialdom inescapably tagged) "an emotionally disturbed segment of the populace," did they turn it over to the Ticktockman and his legal machinery. But by then, because it was the very world it was, and they had no way to predict he would happen— possibly a strain of disease long-defunct, now, suddenly, reborn in a system where immunity had been forgotten, had lapsed—he had been allowed to become too real. Now he had form and substance.

He had become a *personality,* something they had filtered out of the system many decades before. But there it was, and there *he* was, a very definitely imposing personality. In certain circles—middle-class circles—it was thought disgusting. Vulgar ostentation. Anarchistic. Shameful. In others there was only sniggering: those strata where thought is subjugated to form and ritual, niceties, proprieties. But down below, ah, down below, where the people always needed their saints and sinners, their bread and circuses, their heroes and villains, he was considered a Bolivar; a Napoleon; a Robin Hood; a Dick Bong (Ace of Aces); a Jesus; a Jomo Kenyatta.

And at the top—where, like socially-attuned Shipwreck Kellys, every tremor and vibration threatening to dislodge the wealthy, powerful and titled from their flagpoles—he was considered a menace; a heretic; a rebel; a disgrace; a peril. He was known down the line, to the very heart-meat core, but the important reactions were high above and far below. At the very top, at the very bottom.

So his file was turned over, along with his time-card and his cardioplate, to the office of the Ticktockman.

The Ticktockman: very much over six feet tall, often silent, a soft purring man when things went timewise. The Ticktockman.

Even in the cubicles of the hierarchy, where fear was generated, seldom suffered, he was called the Ticktockman. But no one called him that to his mask.

You don't call a man a hated name, not when that man, behind his mask, is capable of revoking the minutes, the hours, the days and nights, the years of your life. He was called the Master Timekeeper to his mask. It was safer that way.

"That is *what* he is," said the Ticktockman with genuine softness, "but not *who* he is. This time-card I'm holding in my left hand has a name on it, but it is the name of *what* he is, not *who* he is. The cardioplate here in my right hand is also named, but not *whom* named, merely *what* named. Before I can exercise proper revocation, I have to

know *who* this *what* is."

To his staff, all the ferrets, all the loggers, all the finks, all the commex, even the mineez, he said, "Who is the Harlequin?"

He was not purring smoothly. Timewise, it was a jangle.

However, it was the longest speech they had ever heard him utter at one time, the staff, the ferrets, the loggers, the finks, the commex, but not the mineez, who usually weren't around to know, in any case. But even they scurried to find out.

Who is the Harlequin?

High above the third level of the city, he crouched on the humming aluminum-frame platform of the air-boat (foof! air-boat, indeed! swizzleskid is what it was, with a tow-rack jerry-rigged) and he stared down at the neat Mondrian arrangement of the buildings.

Somewhere nearby, he could hear the metronomic left-right-left of the 2:47 PM shift, entering the Timkin roller-bearing plant in their sneakers. A minute later, precisely, he heard the softer right-left-right of the 5:00 AM formation, going home.

An elfin grin spread across his tanned features, and his dimples appeared for a moment. Then, scratching at his thatch of auburn hair, he shrugged within his motley, as though girding himself for what came next, and threw the joystick forward, and bent into the wind as the air-boat dropped. He skimmed over a slidewalk, purposely dropping a few feet to crease the tassels of the ladies of fashion, and—inserting thumbs in large ears—he stuck out his tongue, rolled his eyes and went wugga-wugga-wugga. It was a minor diversion. One pedestrian skittered and tumbled, sending parcels everywhichway, another wet herself, a third keeled slantwise and the walk was stopped automatically by the servitors till she could be resuscitated. It was a minor diversion.

Then he swirled away on a vagrant breeze, and was gone. Hi-ho.

As he rounded the cornice of the Time-Motion Study Building, he saw the shift, just boarding the slidewalk. With practiced motion and an absolute conservation of movement, they sidestepped up onto the slow-strip and (in a chorus line reminiscent of a Busby Berkeley film of the antediluvian 1930s) advanced across the strips ostrich-walking till they were lined up on the expresstrip.

Once more, in anticipation, the elfin grin spread, and there was a tooth missing back there on the left side. He dipped, skimmed, and swooped over them; and then, scrunching about on the air-boat, he released the holding pins that fastened shut the ends of the home-made pouring troughs that kept his cargo from dumping prematurely. And as he pulled the trough-pins, the air-boat slid over the factory workers and one hundred and fifty thousand dollars' worth of jelly beans cascaded down on the expresstrip.

Jelly beans! Millions and billions of purples and yellows and greens and licorice and grape and raspberry and mint and round and smooth and crunchy outside and soft-mealy inside and sugary and bouncing jouncing tumbling clittering clattering skittering fell on the heads and shoulders and hardhats and carapaces of the Timkin workers, tinkling on the slidewalk and bouncing away and rolling about underfoot and filling the sky on their way down with all the colors of joy and childhood and holidays, coming down in a steady rain, a solid wash, a torrent of color and sweetness out of the sky from above, and entering a universe of sanity and metronomic order with quite-mad coocoo newness. Jelly beans!

The shift workers howled and laughed and were pelted, and broke ranks, and the jelly beans managed to work their way into the mechanism of the slidewalks after which there was a hideous scraping as the sound of a million fingernails rasped down a quarter of a million blackboards, followed by a coughing and a sputtering, and then the slidewalks all stopped and everyone was dumped thisawayandthataway in a jackstraw tumble, still laughing and popping little jelly bean eggs of childish color into their mouths. It was a holiday, and a jollity, an absolute insanity, a giggle. But . . .

The shift was delayed seven minutes.

They did not get home for seven minutes.

The master schedule was thrown off by seven minutes.

Quotas were delayed by inoperative slidewalks for seven minutes.

He had tapped the first domino in the line, and one after another, like chik chik chik, the others had fallen.

The System had been seven minutes' worth of disrupted. It was a tiny matter, one hardly worthy of note, but in a society where the single driving force was order and unity and equality and promptness and clocklike precision and attention to the clock, reverence of the gods of the passage of time, it was a disaster of major importance.

So he was ordered to appear before the Ticktockman. It was broadcast across every channel of the communications web. He was ordered to be *there* at 7:00 dammit on time. And they waited, and they waited, but he didn't show up till almost ten-thirty, at which time he merely sang a little song about moonlight in a place no one had ever heard of, called Vermont, and vanished once again. But they had all been waiting since seven, and it wrecked *hell* with their schedules. So the question remained: Who is the Harlequin?

But the *unasked* question (more important of the two) was: how did we get *into* this position, where a laughing, irresponsible japer of jabberwocky and jive could disrupt our entire economic and cultural life with a hundred and fifty thousand dollars' worth of jelly beans...

Jelly for God's sake *beans*! This is madness! Where did he get the money to buy a hundred and fifty thousand dollars' worth of jelly beans? (They knew it would have cost that much, because they had a team of Situation Analysts pulled off another assignment, and rushed to the slidewalk scene to sweep up and count the candies, and produce findings, which disrupted *their* schedules and threw their entire branch at least a day behind.) Jelly beans! Jelly... *beans*? Now wait a second—a second accounted for—no one has manufactured jelly beans for over a hundred years. Where did he get jelly beans?

That's another good question. More than likely it will never be answered to your complete satisfaction. But then, how many questions ever are?

The middle you know. Here is the beginning. How it starts.

A desk pad. Day for day, and turn each day. 9:00—open the mail. 9:45—appointment with planning commission board. 10:30—discuss installation progress charts with J.L. 11:45—pray for rain. 12:00—lunch. *And so it goes.*

"I'm sorry, Miss Grant, but the time for interviews was set at 2:30, and it's almost five now. I'm sorry you're late, but those are the rules. You'll have to wait till next year to submit application for this college again." *And so it goes.*

The 10:10 local stops a Cresthaven, Galesville, Tonawanda Junction,

Selby and Farnhurst, but not at Indiana City, Lucasville and Colton, except on Sunday. The 10:35 express stops at Galesville, Selby and Indiana City, except on Sundays & Holidays, at which time it stops at . . . *and so it goes.*

"I couldn't wait, Fred. I had to be a Pierre Cartain's by 3:00, and you said you'd meet me under the clock in the terminal at 2:45, and you weren't there, so I had to go on. You're always late, Fred. If you'd been there, we could have sewed it up together, but as it was, well, I took the order alone. . ." ***And so it goes.***

Dear Mr. and Mrs. Atterley: In reference to your son Gerold's constant tardiness, I am afraid we will have to suspend him from school unless some more reliable method can be instituted guaranteeing he will arrive at his classes on time. Granted he is an exemplary student, and his marks are high, his constant flouting of the schedules of this school makes it impractical to maintain him in a system where the other children seem capable of getting where they are supposed to be on time ***and so it goes.***

YOU CANNOT VOTE UNLESS YOU APPEAR AT 8:45 AM.

"I don't care if the script is *good*, I need it Thursday!"

CHECK-OUT TIME IS 2:00 PM.

"You got here late. The job is taken. Sorry."

YOUR SALARY HAS BEEN DOCKED FOR TWENTY MINUTES TIME LOST.

"God, what time is it, I've gotta run!"

And so it goes. And so it goes. And so it goes. And so it goes goes

goes goes goes tick tock tick tock tick tock and one day we no longer let time serve us, we serve time and we are slaves of the schedule, worshippers of the sun's passing, bound into a life predicated on restrictions because the system will not function if we don't keep the schedule tight.

Until it becomes more than a minor inconvenience to be late. It becomes a sin. Then a crime. Then a crime punishable by this:

EFFECTIVE 15 JULY 2389 12:00:00 midnight, the office of the Master Timekeeper will require all citizens to submit their time-cards and cardioplates for processing. In accordance with Statute 555-7-SGH-999 governing the revocation of time per capita, all cardioplates will be keyed to the individual holder and—

What they had done was devise a method of curtailing the amount of life a person could have. If he was ten minutes late, he lost ten minutes of his life. An hour was proportionately worth more revocation. If someone was consistently tardy, he might find himself, on a Sunday night, receiving a communiqué from the Master Timekeeper that his time had run out, and he would be "turned off" at high noon on Monday, please straighten your affairs, sir, madame or bisex.

And so, by this simple scientific expedient (utilizing a scientific process held dearly secret by the Ticktockman's office) the System was maintained. It was the only expedient thing to do. It was, after all,

patriotic. The schedules had to be met. After all, there *was* a war on!

But, wasn't there always?

"Now that is really disgusting," the Harlequin said, when pretty Alice showed him the wanted poster. "Disgusting and *highly* improbable. After all, this isn't the Day of the Desperado. A *wanted* poster!"

"You know," Pretty Alice noted, "you speak with a great deal of inflection."

"I'm sorry," said the Harlequin, humbly.

"No need to be sorry. You're always saying 'I'm sorry.' You have such massive guilt, Everett, it's really very sad."

"I'm sorry," he said again, then pursed his lips so the dimples appeared momentarily. He hadn't wanted to say that at all. "I have to go out again. I have to *do* something."

Pretty Alice slammed her coffee-bulb down on the counter. "Oh for God's *sake*, Everett, can't you stay home just *one* night! Must you always be out in that ghastly clown suit, running around an*noy*ing people?"

"I'm—" He stopped, and clapped the jester's hat onto his auburn thatch with a tiny tingling of bells. He rose, rinsed out his coffee-bulb at the spray, and put it into the dryer for a moment. "I have to go."

She didn't answer. The faxbox was purring, and she pulled a sheet out, read it, threw it toward him on the counter. "It's about you. Of course. You're ridiculous."

He read it quickly. It said the Ticktockman was trying to locate him. He didn't care, he was going out to be late again. At the door, dredging for an exit line, he hurled back petulantly, "Well, *you* speak with inflection, *too*!"

Pretty Alice rolled her pretty eyes heavenward. "You're ridiculous." The Harlequin stalked out, slamming the door, which sighed shut softly, and locked itself.

There was gentle knock, and Pretty Alice got up with an exhalation of exasperated breath, and opened the door. He stood there. "I'll be back about ten-thirty, okay?"

She pulled a rueful face. "Why do you tell me that? Why? You *know* you'll be late! You *know* it! You're *always* late, so why do you tell me these dumb things?" She closed the door.

On the other side, the Harlequin nodded to himself. *She's right. She's always right. I'll be late. I'm always late. Why do I tell her these dumb things?*

He shrugged again, and went off to be late once more.

He had fired off the firecracker rockets that said: **I will attend the 115th annual International Medical Association Invocation at**

8:00 PM precisely. I do hope you will all be able to join me.

The words had burned in the sky, and of course the authorities were there, lying in wait for him. They assumed, naturally, that he would be late. He arrived twenty minutes early, while they were setting up the spiderwebs to trap and hold him. Blowing a large bullhorn, he frightened and unnerved them so, their own moisturized encirclement webs sucked closed, and they were hauled up, kicking and shrieking, high above the amphitheater's floor. The Harlequin laughed and laughed, and apologized profusely. The physicians, gathered in solemn conclave, roared with laughter, and accepted the Harlequin's apologies with exaggerated bowing and posturing, and a merry time was had by all, who thought the Harlequin was a regular foofaraw in fancy pants; all, that is, but the authorities, who had been sent out by the office of the Ticktockman; they hung there like so much dockside cargo, hauled up above the floor of the amphitheater in a most unseemly fashion.

(In another part of the same city where the Harlequin carried on his "activities," totally unrelated in every way to what concerns us here, save that it illustrates the Ticktockman's power and import, a man named Marshall Delahanty received his turn-off notice from the Ticktockman's office. His wife received the notification from the gray-suited minee who delivered it, with the traditional "look of sorrow" plastered hideously across his face. She knew what it was, even without unsealing it. It was a billet-doux of immediate recognition to everyone these days. She gasped, and held it as though it were a glass slide tinged with botulism, and prayed it was not for her. Let it be for Marsh, she thought, brutally, realistically, or one of the kids, but not for me, please dear God, not for me. And then she opened it, and it *was* for Marsh, and she was at one and the same time horrified and relieved. The next trooper in the line had caught the bullet. "Marshall," she screamed, "Marshall! Termination, Marshall! OhmiGod, Marshall, whattl we do, whattl we do, Marshall omigodmarshall . . ." and in their home that night was the sound of tearing paper and fear, and the stink of madness went up the flue and there was nothing, absolutely nothing they could do about it.

(But Marshall Delahanty tried to run. And early the next day, when turn-off time came, he was deep in the Canadian forest two hundred miles away, and the office of the Ticktockman blanked his cardioplate, and Marshall Delahanty keeled over, running, and his heart stopped, and the blood dried up on its way to his brain, and he was dead that's all. One light went out on the sector map in the office of the Master Timekeeper, while notification was entered for fax reproduction, and Georgette Delahanty's name was entered on the dole roles till she could remarry. Which is the end of the footnote, and all the point that

need be made, except don't laugh, because that is what would happen to the Harlequin if ever the Ticktockman found out his real name. It isn't funny.)

The shopping level of the city was thronged with the Thursdaycolors of the buyers. Women in canary yellow chitons and men in pseudo-Tyrolean outfits that were jade and leather and fit very tightly, save for the balloon pants.

When the Harlequin appeared on the still-being-constructed shell of the new Efficiency Shopping Center, his bullhorn to his elfishly-laughing lips, everyone pointed and stared, and he berated them:

"Why let them order you about? Why let them tell you to hurry and scurry like ants or maggots? Take your time! Saunter a while! Enjoy the sunshine, enjoy the breeze, let life carry you at your own pace! Don't be slaves of time, it's a helluva way to die, slowly, by degrees. . . down with the Ticktockman!"

Who's the nut? most of the shoppers wanted to know. Who's the nut oh wow I'm gonna be late I gotta run. . .

And the construction gang on the Shopping Center received an urgent order from the office of the Master Timekeeper that the dangerous criminal known as the Harlequin was atop their spire, and their aid was urgently needed in apprehending him. The work crew said no, they would lose time on their construction schedule, but the Ticktockman managed to pull the proper threads of governmental webbing, and they were told to cease work and catch that nitwit up there on the spire; up there with the bullhorn. So a dozen and more burly workers began climbing into their construction platforms, releasing the a-grav plates, and rising toward the Harlequin.

After the debacle (in which, through the Harlequin's attention to personal safety, no one was seriously injured), the workers tried to reassemble, and assault him again, but it was too late. He had vanished. It had attracted quite a crowd, however, and the shopping cycle was thrown off by hours, simply hours. The purchasing needs of the system were therefore falling behind, and so measures were taken to accelerate the cycle for the rest of the day, but it got bogged down and speeded up and they sold too many float-valves and not nearly enough wegglers, which meant that the popli ratio was off, which made it necessary to rush cases and cases of spoiling Smash-O to stores that usually needed a case only every three or four hours. The shipments were bollixed, the transshipments were misrouted, and in the end, even the swizzleskid industries felt it.

"Don't come back till you have him!" the Ticktockman said, very quietly, very sincerely, extremely dangerously.

They used dogs. They used probes. They used cardioplate crossoffs. They used teepers. They used bribery. They used stiktytes. They used intimidation. They used torment. They used torture. They used finks. They used cops. They used search&seizure. They used fallaron. They used betterment incentive. They used fingerprints. They used the Bertillon system. They used cunning. They used guile. They used treachery. They used Raoul Mitgong, but he didn't help much. They used applied physics. They used techniques of criminology.

And what the hell: they caught him.

After all, his name was Everett C. Marm, and he wasn't much to begin with, except a man who had no sense of time.

"Repent, Harlequin!" said the Ticktockman.

"Get stuffed!" the Harlequin replied, sneering.

"You've been late a total of sixty-three years, five months, three weeks, two days, twelve hours, forty-one minutes, fifty-nine seconds, point oh three six one one one microseconds. You've used up everything you can, and more. I'm going to turn you off."

"Scare someone else. I'd rather be dead than live in a dumb world with a bogeyman like you."

"It's my job."

"You're full of it. You're a tyrant. You have no right to order people around and kill them if they show up late."

"You can't adjust. You can't fit in."

"Unstrap me, and I'll fit my fist into your mouth."

"You're a nonconformist."

"That didn't used to be a felony."

"It is now. Live in the world around you."

"I hate it. It's a terrible world."

"Not everyone thinks so. Most people enjoy order."

"I don't, and most of the people I know don't."

"That's not true. How do you think we caught you?"

"I'm not interested."

"A girl named Pretty Alice told us who you were."

"That's a lie."

"It's true. You unnerve her. She wants to belong; she wants to conform; I'm going to turn you off."

"Then do it already, and stop arguing with me."

"I'm not going to turn you off."

"You're an idiot!"

"Repent, Harlequin!" said the Ticktockman.

"Get stuffed."

So they sent him to Coventry. And in Coventry they worked him over. It was just like what they did to Winston Smith in NINETEEN EIGHTY-FOUR, which was a book none of them knew about, but the techniques are really quite ancient, and so they did it to Everett C. Marm; and one day, quite a long time later, the Harlequin appeared on the communications web, appearing elfin and dimpled and bright-eyed, and not at all brainwashed, and he said he had been wrong, that it was a good, a very good thing indeed, to belong, to be right on time hip-ho and away we go, and everyone stared up at him on the public screens that covered an entire city block, and they said to themselves, well, you see, he was just a nut after all, and if that's the way the system is run, then let's do it that way, because it doesn't pay to fight city hall, or in this case, the Ticktockman. So Everett C. Marm was destroyed, which was a loss, because of what Thoreau said earlier, but you can't make an omelet without breaking a few eggs, and in every revolution a few die who shouldn't, but they have to, because that's the way it happens, and if you make only a little change, then it seems to be worthwhile. Or, to make the point lucidly:

"Uh, excuse me, sir, I, uh, don't know how to uh, to uh, tell you this, but you were three minutes late. The schedule is a little, uh, bit off."

He grinned sheepishly.

"That's ridiculous!" murmured the Ticktockman behind his mask. "Check your watch." And then he went into his office, going *mrmee, mrmee, mrmee, mrmee.*

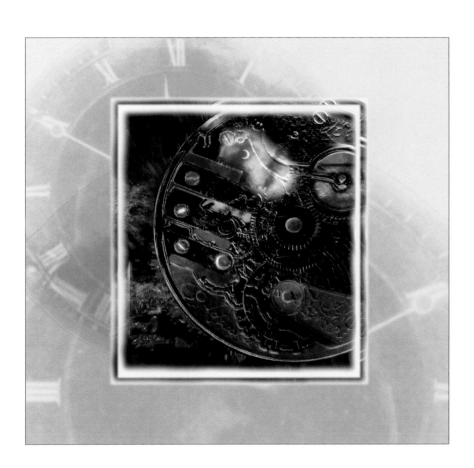

I think I hear him coming back now. My soul, that cutthroat, lunatic masked privateer. If any of you out there can hear me, if any of you out there have been able to untangle my hysterical ravings—and only living trapped in here with a mad soul has made me hysterical, I assure you—please help me.

If you think I like being dragged along on his raids, if you think I like people calling me a troublemaker, if you think I like seeing perfectly sane and rational and orderly people staring at me as though I should be in a straitjacket, if you think I enjoy this miserable life of danger and being out of step...

Tweeeedle-deeee-mrmee, mrmee, mrmee...

THIS IS THE VOICE OF THE SOUL. NOW HEAR THIS:

He may not like it, li'l suckah may not like it at all; but it's the only game in town.

This is the 72nd book **Harlan Ellison** has written or edited; more than 1700 stories, essays, and articles; as well as dozens of screenplays and teleplays. He has won two Mystery Writers of America Edgars, three Horror Writers Association Bram Stoker Awards, multiple Nebula and Hugo awards, the World Fantasy Lifetime Achievement Award, and the Silver Pen for Journalism from PEN, among a plethora of other honors. Ellison's "The Man Who Rowed Christopher Columbus Ashore" was selected for inclusion in the prestigious *The Best American Short Stories* and his book *Angry Candy* was selected by the *Yearbook* of the *Encyclopedia Americana* as one of only twenty-four short-story collections considered "Major Works of American Literature for 1988." He appears as a regular onscreen commentator on the USA Network's Sci-Fi Channel, is Conceptual Consultant on *Babylon 5*, and lives in California with his wife, Susan.

Acknowledged as the creator of the first computer-generated book cover (for William Gibson's *Neuromancer*), **Rick Berry** is an accomplished traditional painter as well and has received numerous awards for his work. His art has been collected in *Double Memory: Art and Collaborations* by Berry and Phil Hale and he teaches design and illustration at Tufts University in Boston. Berry lives with his wife, Sheila, and three children in Massachusetts.

Arnie Fenner is one of the creators responsible for the *Spectrum* series of books that celebrates the best in contemporary fantastic art each year. He has painted covers for and designed the interiors of an impressive variety of books and has received two World Fantasy Awards among many other honors. Fenner lives in Kansas with his wife, Cathy.